Shanté Keys
and the
New Year's
Peas

Gail Piernas-Davenport   illustrated by **Marion Eldridge**

ALBERT WHITMAN & COMPANY
CHICAGO, ILLINOIS

To my family, who believed in my dream, and my writing family, who taught me
how to make it come true—GP-D

To my husband, Paul, with love and gratitude for all his support—ME

Library of Congress Cataloging-in-Publication Data

Piernas-Davenport, Gail.
Shanté Keys and the New Year's peas / by Gail Piernas-Davenport ;
illustrated by Marion Eldridge.
p. cm.
Summary: When Shanté is sent to find black-eyed peas for her family's New Year's
celebration, she learns about each of her neighbor's New Year's traditions in their
home countries.
[1. New Year—Fiction. 2. Peas—Fiction. 3. Stories in rhyme.]
I. Eldridge, Marion, ill. II. Title.
PZ8.3.P5586435Sh 2007 [E]—dc22 2007001349

Printed in China
10 9 8 7 6 5 4 WKT 26 25 24 23 22 21

For more information about Albert Whitman & Company,
visit our website at www.albertwhitman.com.

"Happy New Year, Grandma!" says Shanté Keys.
"Mom said we'll eat lucky New Year's peas."

"Mercy!" cries Grandma.
"I'm weak in the knees.
I cooked lots of food,
but forgot black-eyed peas!

"Chitlins, baked ham,
macaroni and cheese,
greens and hot corn bread,
but no black-eyed peas!"

"It's a year of bad luck if we don't eat cowpeas.
Quick—go to Miss Lee's and borrow some, please!"

"Happy New Year, Miss Lee," says Shanté Keys.
"Gram wants to borrow some black-eyed peas."

"My New Year is later because I'm Chinese.
I'll make crisp golden dumplings instead of cowpeas."

"I'm sorry to bother you," says Shanté Keys.
"Come join us for dinner so you can try peas.

"I'll try at the grocer's—
Mr. MacGhee's."

"Your aisles are stocked with such delicacies. Why can't I find lucky black-eyed peas?"

"Back home in my Scotland, far overseas,
for New Year's we toast and eat haggis and cheese."

"Happy New Year, anyway," says Shanté Keys.
"Come join us for dinner so you can try peas."

"Why don't you try asking Señor Ortiz?"

"What do you eat for New Year's luck, Chef Ortiz?
If you cook blackeyes, may I borrow some, please?"

"I am from Mexico, down by Belize.
For luck, we make noise and eat grapes like these."

"Happy New Year, anyway," says Shanté Keys.
"Come join us for dinner so you can try peas."

Next Shanté asks at her good friend Hari's.
"May I borrow peas for New Year's, please?"

"We celebrate Diwali with other Hindu families.
We light lamps and eat sweets—but no black-eyed peas."

"Thank you, anyway," says Shanté Keys.
"Come join us for dinner so you can try peas."

Now Shanté is frantic; she's in a time squeeze.
She thinks hard and rushes to Auntie Marie's.

"I'd have too many if I cooked all of these.
Hon, take what you need of my New Year's peas."

"Thanks, and come eat at Gram's with me, please!"

Grandma chops onions to cook with the peas.
Auntie adds a coin for luck and a pinch of bay leaves.

And Shanté cooks rice as Mom oversees.

Auntie says, "Shanté, can you get the door, please?"
Your friends are here for dinner, come to try peas!"

"The peas are delicious!" the whole group agrees.
"Happy New Year and thank you, Shanté Keys!"

LUCKY FOOD?
ABOUT NEW YEAR'S TRADITIONS

Like the Keys family, many African Americans and people from the southern United States believe eating black-eyed peas on January 1 will bring good luck and prosperity for the new year. This has been a custom since the Civil War. Sometimes a dime is added to the pot, or else a penny is placed under the pot when the dish is served. Black-eyed peas (also known as blackeye peas or cowpeas) are thought by many to symbolize pennies, while others believe that peas mean peace in the new year.

Traditionally, black-eyed peas are cooked with ham hocks, bacon slices, or salt pork and served with rice in a dish called Hoppin' John. It's often served with greens—which represent folding money—and corn bread, which stands for gold.

Other parts of the world celebrate the new year with different foods and customs, and even on different calendars. The Chinese New Year is based on the lunar calendar; it begins between late January and the middle of February on the second new moon after winter starts and lasts for fifteen days. People clean their homes to avoid bad luck in the new year and make homemade dumplings called jiaozi. When fried, they are crusty and golden brown, representing golden coins and wishes for prosperity.

In Scotland, New Year's has a long tradition as a favorite holiday. The Scottish celebration is called Hogmanay. Everyone raises a glass to toast the new year—even the children, who drink ginger wine, which is like ginger ale. The new year's meal consists of cold meats, haggis (stuffed sheep's stomach), "bashed neeps and tatties" (mashed turnips and potatoes), cheese, cakes, and scones. Three-cornered biscuits called hogmanays are also served. People sing the traditional new year's song, "Auld Lang Syne," which was written by a Scot, Robert Burns. "Auld Lang Syne" means "The Good Old Days."

Midnight on New Year's Eve in many Spanish-speaking countries is a busy—and noisy—time. Families throw buckets of water out into the street to symbolize a clean start for the new year. Fireworks and firecrackers are set off too. At midnight, everyone eats twelve grapes to symbolize twelve months of good fortune. One grape must be eaten at each chime of the clock, so you have to eat fast!

In northern India, the Hindu New Year of Diwali, the Festival of Lights, begins in October or November and is celebrated for five days, each day honoring a different Hindu god or goddess. This holiday is as important to Hindus as Christmas is to Christians. Families make intricate drawings called rangoli with colored rice powder on the sidewalks outside their homes. Sweets, especially those made from milk like barfi, ladoo, and cham cham, are shared with friends and taken to the temple to honor the god Rama and his wife, Sita. Houses are lit with oil lamps called diyas or strings of electric lights and fireworks light the sky.

WHAT OTHER FOODS HAVE SPECIAL MEANING AT THE NEW YEAR?

Austria: Roast suckling pig is eaten for good luck. Crayfish and lobster symbolize bad luck and are not served, because these animals move backward and are thought to be looking to the past.

Germany: December 31 is also known as Saint Sylvester's Eve here. Carp is a traditional dish, and a scale of the fish is saved as a good-luck charm for the new year.

Greece: On January 1, the feast of Saint Basil, special Saint Basil's cakes are made. Each one is covered in almonds and walnuts and has a coin baked inside for a lucky child to discover. Greeks believe if you eat something sweet, you will have a sweet year!

Japan: The new year is called Oshogatsu in Japan. A popular custom is to eat thin buckwheat noodles called soba, which represent long life. To bring luck, children try to swallow one noodle whole without chewing it.

Jewish New Year: At Rosh Hashanah, which begins in September or October, sliced apples are dipped into honey to make a sweet new year.

Korea: For Solnal, the lunar new year, Koreans eat rice cake soup, Ttokkuk, to ward off illness and mark another year of life.

Switzerland: The Swiss believe a drop of cream fallen to the floor will bring luck.

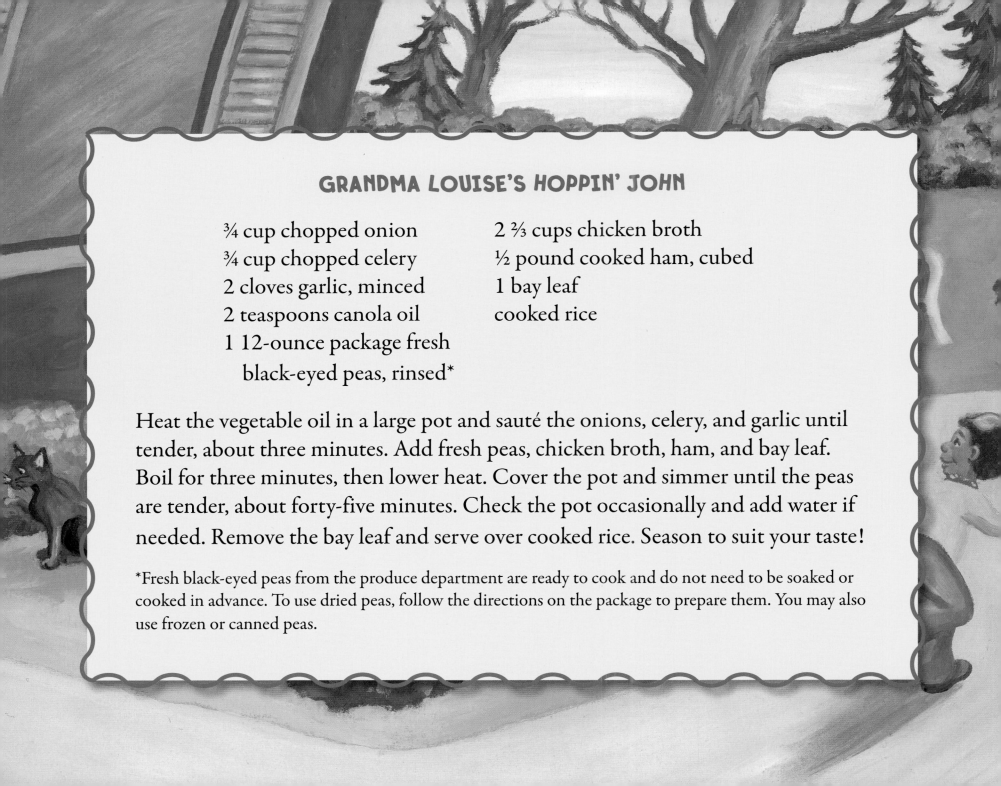

GRANDMA LOUISE'S *HOPPIN' JOHN*

¾ cup chopped onion

¾ cup chopped celery

2 cloves garlic, minced

2 teaspoons canola oil

1 12-ounce package fresh
    black-eyed peas, rinsed*

2 ⅔ cups chicken broth

½ pound cooked ham, cubed

1 bay leaf

cooked rice

Heat the vegetable oil in a large pot and sauté the onions, celery, and garlic until tender, about three minutes. Add fresh peas, chicken broth, ham, and bay leaf. Boil for three minutes, then lower heat. Cover the pot and simmer until the peas are tender, about forty-five minutes. Check the pot occasionally and add water if needed. Remove the bay leaf and serve over cooked rice. Season to suit your taste!

*Fresh black-eyed peas from the produce department are ready to cook and do not need to be soaked or cooked in advance. To use dried peas, follow the directions on the package to prepare them. You may also use frozen or canned peas.